D0099873

Brown, Marc Tolon.
Arthur's computer
disaster /
c1997.
33305011495672
GI   05/06/99

MARC BROWN

Little, Brown and Company

Boston   New York   Toronto   London

SANTA CLARA COUNTY LIBRARY

3 3305 01149 5672

For
Eliza Morgan Brown

Copyright © 1997 by Marc Brown

All rights reserved. No part of this book may be reproduced
in any form or by any electronic or mechanical means,
including information storage and retrieval systems, without
permission in writing from the publisher, except
by a reviewer who may quote brief passages in a review.

First Edition

Adapted by Marc Brown
from a teleplay by Joe Fallon

Brown, Marc, Tolon.
    Arthur's computer disaster/Marc Brown. — 1st ed.
        p.   cm.
    Summary: Arthur disobeys his mother by playing his favorite game
on her computer, which leads to a lesson in taking responsibility
for one's actions.
    ISBN 0-316-11016-7
    [1. Computer games — Fiction.   2. Responsibility — Fiction.]
I. Title.
PZ7.B81618A1n   1997
[E] — dc20   96-42418

        10 9 8 7 6 5 4

                WOR

Published simultaneously in Canada
by Little, Brown & Company (Canada) Limited

Printed in the United States of America

"Mom, can I use your computer to play Deep, Dark Sea?" asked Arthur.
"What's Deep, Dark Sea?" asked D.W.
"Only the greatest game in the universe," said Arthur.
"Can I, Mom, please?"

"What's the game about?" asked D.W.
"A haunted sunken ship," said Arthur.
"With skeletons, ghosts, and sharks."
"Sounds spooky," said D.W.

"Mom, please," begged Arthur.
"Oh, all right," said Mom, "but finish your dinner first."
Arthur finished his dinner in a jiffy.

Once Arthur started playing Deep, Dark Sea,
he couldn't stop.
"Time for bed," said Dad.
"But Dad, I almost found *the thing*," said Arthur.

"When I find *the thing*, I can win stuff."
"You can find *the thing* tomorrow," said Dad.
"It's bedtime."
"I'm ready for bed," said D.W. sweetly.

The next morning, Buster came over to play
Deep, Dark Sea.
"Sorry, boys," said Mom. "It's tax season.
I need my computer all day."

Just then the phone rang. It was for Mom.
"I have to run to the office," she said. "And don't touch
my computer."

After Mom left, Arthur and Buster stared at
the computer.

"I know what you're thinking," said D.W.

"But I'm so close to finding *the thing,*" said Arthur.

"You could probably find it before your mom gets home,"
said Buster.

"I'm telling Dad," warned D.W.

"I'll give you my desserts for a whole week," said Arthur.

"And play dollhouse with me whenever I say so?"
asked D.W.

"Yes," grumbled Arthur.

"And call me Your Royal Highness…?" asked D.W.

"Don't push it," said Arthur.

Arthur loaded the game.
"Look out for the Squid Squad!" yelled Buster.
"I'm running out of oxygen," said Arthur.
"Look," said Buster. "A treasure chest!"

Just then the phone rang. Everyone jumped.
It was Mom.
"I won't be home until tonight," she said. "Everything all right?"
"Umm, fine, just great," said Arthur.
"You know, Mom can tell when you're lying," whispered D.W.
"Maybe we can fix it before she gets home," said Arthur.

The keyboard crashed to the floor.
"Uh-oh," said Arthur.
"You're in big trouble," said D.W.

"That's it!" screamed Arthur. "That's *the thing!* I found it!"
"Let me open it!" shouted Buster.
"I found it," argued Arthur.
They both dove for the mouse.

Arthur looked through the computer manual.
"There's nothing in here about Deep, Dark Sea
accidents," he said.
"Are you sure you have the right manual?" asked D.W.

"The Brain can fix anything," said Buster. "Let's ask him."
"Alan's not home," said the Brain's mom.

They checked the library.

They checked the museum.
Just when they were about to give up, they found him.

"Are you doing a science experiment?" asked Buster.
"No, I'm skipping stones," said the Brain. "It's fun!"

Everyone went back to Arthur's house.
The Brain examined the computer.
"Hmmm," said the Brain. He shook his head.
"That bad?" asked Arthur.
"It must be," said the Brain. "I can't find the problem."
"Well, thanks for trying," said Arthur.
"Now you're in really, really big trouble," said D.W.
"If the Brain can't fix it, who can?" said Buster.
"I have an idea," said Arthur.

Arthur explained his problem to the computer expert.
Then the computer expert explained how much a house
call and hourly fees would cost.
"That's more birthday money than I'll ever see in my
whole life," said Arthur. "I'm doomed."

"We're all doomed," said D.W. "Because now Mommy will lose her job and we won't be able to keep our house and we'll all have to live in the cold on the street and we'll all get ammonia and probably die and it's all your fault, Arthur!"

That evening, Arthur hardly touched his dinner.
"Hi, I'm home," called Mom.
"Mom, how about a game of cards?" asked Arthur.
"And a family bike ride?"

"Don't have time, sweetie," said Mom. "I have tons of work."
Mom headed for the computer.
Arthur felt sick.

Arthur ran after Mom.
D.W. ran after Arthur.
Buster ran home.

Just as Mom's finger was about to hit the ON button,
Arthur yelled, "Stop!"
"I was playing Deep, Dark Sea, and the screen went
blank. I'm sorry. I wrecked it. It's all my fault."

"That happens to me all the time," said Mom.
"Did you jiggle the switch?"
Mom jiggled the switch, and the game came on.
"Why didn't you call me?" asked Mom.
"Always call me with your problems."
"I thought you'd be mad," said Arthur.
"I'm not mad," said Mom. "I'm disappointed."

"Am I going to get punished?" asked Arthur.
"Of course," said Mom. "You did something you weren't supposed to do."
"Make the punishment really good," said D.W.
"No computer games for a week," said Mom. "Now, get ready for bed. I'll be up to say good night in a few minutes."

Arthur and D.W. did as they were told.
Then they waited for what seemed like a very long time.
"Mom," called Arthur. "Time to tuck us in."

"In a minute," said Mom. "The sharks are attacking!"
"Maybe we should tuck ourselves in tonight," said D.W.
"Good idea," said Arthur.

"I'll be right up," called Mom. "As soon as I blast these skeletons from the treasure chest."

"Good night, Mom," called D.W.
"Good night, Mom," called Arthur.